DINNER at AUNT CONNIE'S HOUSE

To Mrs Middleton
You can fly
Faith Ringgold

DINNER
at AUNT CONNIE'S HOUSE
Faith Ringgold

Hyperion Paperbacks for Children
New York

First Hyperion Paperback edition 1996

Text and illustrations © 1993 by Faith Ringgold.

Printed in Hong Kong

5 7 9 10 8 6 4

Library of Congress Cataloging-in-Publication Data
Ringgold, Faith.
Dinner at Aunt Connie's house / Faith Ringgold / 1st. ed.
p.   cm.
Summary: Dinner at Aunt Connie's is even more special than usual
when Melody meets not only her new adopted cousin but twelve
inspiring African-American women, who step out of their portraits
and join the family for dinner.
ISBN 1-56282-425-2 (trade)—ISBN 1-56282-426-0 (lib. bdg.)
ISBN 0-7868-1150-1 (pbk.)
[1. Afro-Americans—Fiction. 2. Dinners and dining—Fiction.]
I. Title.
PZ7.R4726Di   1993
(E)—dc20   92-54871

My father,

Andrew Louis Jones, Sr.,

who was no feminist, was fond of introducing women he admired as *great*
women. So I grew up knowing that women could be great. I learned later he meant
these women could stand alone and were not afraid to take risks.

My uncle,

Cardoza Bunion Posey,

admired women who were learned. It was he who took me to meet Mary McLeod
Bethune when she came to Harlem in the 1930s.

My mother,

Willi Edell Posey,

a *great woman,* invited Fannie Lou Hamer in 1960 to speak at her fashion show to
raise money for the voter registration drive.

This book is dedicated to all the risk takers and great women in history.
Without them where would women be?

ACKNOWLEDGMENTS
Thanks to my daughter, Barbara Wallace, for the research she did on the women in this book and
to my editor, Andrea Cascardi, for seeing it through its reincarnation from "The Dinner Quilt" to
Dinner at Aunt Connie's House.

—Faith Ringgold, 3/11/93

My aunt Connie is a great artist. She and Uncle Bates live in a big beautiful house on the beach in Sag Harbor, Long Island. Every summer they invite our whole family to come for a delicious dinner and a special showing of Aunt Connie's artwork. I could hardly wait for this year's dinner — not only for the food but also for the art, which was to be a big surprise.

Another surprise was Lonnie, my aunt and uncle's adopted son. I fell in love with him the first time I saw him. Have you ever seen a little black boy with red hair and green eyes? Neither had I before Lonnie. While the rest of the family relaxed on the beach before dinner, Lonnie and I went in the house and played hide-and-seek.

I heard some noises up in the attic and climbed the stairs to see if Lonnie was up there.

"Come out, come out, wherever you are," I sang out.

"Come in, Melody," a strange voice answered. "We would like to talk to you."

"Lonnie, stop trying to scare me with that strange voice," I said.

I peeked into the attic and saw twelve beautiful paintings. I knew I had found Aunt Connie's surprise.

"Lonnie," I yelled, "please come out of your hiding place."

"Melody," Lonnie answered, "I am right beside you, and I heard that strange voice, too."

"Aunt Connie's paintings can talk, Lonnie."

"Paintings don't talk, Melody. Only the artist can speak."

"Yes, we can speak, Lonnie," the voice said.

"Who are you?" we chimed in chorus as we held hands and entered the strange room.

"I will be the first to speak. I am Rosa Parks. I was born in 1913 in Alabama. I am called the mother of the civil rights movement. In 1955, I was arrested for refusing to sit in the back of the bus. That incident started the Montgomery bus boycott and inspired Martin Luther King, Jr., to devote his life to the civil rights movement."

"But how can you speak? Paintings don't talk like people," Lonnie said.

"Your aunt Connie created us to tell you the history of our struggle. Would you like to hear more?"

We nodded, and the next painting spoke.

"I am Fannie Lou Hamer, born in 1917 in Mississippi. I was a civil rights activist and public speaker. I worked with Martin Luther King for voters' rights in the South. I helped thousands of people register to vote."

"My dream was education. I am Mary McLeod Bethune, born in 1875 in South Carolina. I founded Bethune-Cookman College. I was a special adviser to Presidents Franklin D. Roosevelt and Harry S Truman and founded the National Council of Negro Women, an organization that has more than one million members."

"I was a sculptor. My name is Augusta Savage, and I was born in 1892 in Florida. I founded The Savage Studio of Arts and Crafts in Harlem. I taught many artists to paint, draw, and sculpt. Maybe you've heard of one of my students, the famous painter Jacob Lawrence?"

"My name is Dorothy Dandridge. Born in 1922 in Ohio, I was the first African-American actress to become a Hollywood star. I was nominated for an Academy Award in 1954 for Best Actress for the film *Carmen Jones*. I starred in other films with famous actors such as James Mason and Joan Fontaine."

"I am Zora Neale Hurston, born in 1901 in Florida."

"I know who you are," I said. "You're a famous writer."

"Yes, Melody. In the 1930s I was the most prolific African-American writer. My books — *Their Eyes Were Watching God*, *Moses, Man of the Mountain*, and *Mules and Men* — are considered among the best examples of American writing."

"I was born way back in 1803 in Connecticut. My name is Maria W. Stewart. Back then, women could not be public speakers, yet I spoke out for the human rights of oppressed blacks. I was also the first African American to lecture in defense of women's rights."

"I am Bessie Smith, empress of blues. I was born in 1894 in Tennessee. I was once the highest paid African-American artist in the world. The great jazz trumpeter Louis Armstrong was one of my accompanists. I inspired many singers with my soul and spirit."

"People called me Moses. I am Harriet Tubman, born in 1820 in Maryland. I brought more than three hundred slaves to freedom in the North in nineteen trips on the Underground Railroad — and never lost a passenger. Among them were my aged mother and father and my ten brothers and sisters."

"I am Sojourner Truth, born in 1797 in New York State. I was an itinerant preacher and an abolitionist with Frederick Douglass and William Lloyd Garrison. I spoke out for women's rights during slavery, when no American woman had the right to vote. I met and spoke with President Abraham Lincoln."

"I am Marian Anderson,
born in 1902 in Pennsylvania.
Arturo Toscanini, the great conductor, said a voice such as mine
is heard only once in a hundred years. I was denied the right to sing at Constitution
Hall by the Daughters of the American Revolution in Washington, D.C. In protest, I sang
on the steps of the Lincoln Memorial to a crowd of 75,000. I was known as the world's greatest living
contralto and was the first African American to perform with the Metropolitan Opera Company."
"Someday I want to be an opera singer, too," Lonnie said.

"My name is Madame C. J. Walker. I was born in 1867 in Louisiana. I was the first self-made American woman millionaire. I employed more than three thousand people in my cosmetics company. My invention, the hair-straightening comb, changed the appearance of millions of people."

"What do you think of us, children?" the paintings asked.

"I am very proud to be an African-American woman," I said.

"You are only a nine year old, Melody, not a woman," Lonnie said.

"And who do you think you are, Lonnie, with your red hair and green eyes? Not many African Americans look like you!"

"My hair is red and my eyes are green, but I am black, ten years old, and just as proud as you to be African American!"

Just then Uncle Bates appeared at the attic door.

"Since you two have already discovered Aunt Connie's surprise, you can help me take the paintings down to hang in the dining room."

Lonnie and I helped Uncle Bates hang the paintings on the dining room walls, then Aunt Connie called the family to dinner to see the big surprise.

Grandpa Bates was our family's toastmaster. Last year he toasted my sister Dee Dee and her fiancé, Carl's, engagement. Today he toasted Lonnie, who was Aunt Connie and Uncle Bates's son from now on. Then Lonnie read an African proverb in Swahili: *"Mti mzuri huota kwenye miiba,"* "A good tree grows among thorns." Aunt Connie's smile told us she knew we had been talking to the paintings.

Lonnie and I winked back at her, keeping the secret.

Aunt Connie's dinners are the best. We had roast turkey, duck, cranberry sauce, corn bread, stuffing, macaroni and cheese, candied sweet potatoes, and fresh greens. Seated around the table were the usual people: Aunt Connie and Uncle Bates, my mother and father, Grandma and Grandpa Bates, my sister Dee Dee and her new husband, Carl, and Mr. and Mrs. Tucker. But only Lonnie and I knew that today's dinner was extra special. It was magical. As we ate, Aunt Connie spoke about each of the women in her portraits.

Aunt Connie's paintings were no longer hanging on the dining room walls but sitting in the chairs around the table as our dinner guests. Aunt Connie's voice faded into the background, and our family disappeared as Sojourner Truth spoke in support of the women's vote:

"Look at me....I have plowed and planted and gathered into barns and no man could head me....I have borne thirteen children and seen most all sold into slavery, and when I cried out a mother's grief, none but Jesus heard me. And ain't I a woman?"

Harriet Tubman spoke about slavery: "There was one of two things I had a right to, liberty or death; if I could not have one, I would have the other, for no man should take me alive."

Maria Stewart spoke next, about a woman's right to speak in public. "Men of eminence have mostly risen from obscurity; nor will I, although female of a darker hue and far more obscure than they, bend my head or hang my harp upon willows, for though poor I will virtuous prove."

"Connie, your art is a great inspiration to us all," said Uncle Bates.

"Their lives speak more powerfully than any paintings could," Aunt Connie said. "Don't you think so children?" She winked her eye at Lonnie and me.

"When I grow up, I want to sing in opera houses all over the world. I know it will be hard, but not as hard for me as it was for Marian Anderson," said Lonnie.

"I want to be president of the United States when I grow up," I said, "so I can change some of the things that make people's lives so sad. I know I can do it because of these women."

"Amen! Amen!" everybody chimed.

"I never thought my wife and the mother of our children would be the president of the United States," Lonnie whispered in my ear.

"And I never thought I would marry an African-American opera singer with red hair and green eyes," I whispered back.

"But what will our children think of Aunt Connie's secret, Melody?"

"Our children will love the secret. We will have delicious family dinners, and they will be magical just like Aunt Connie's, and our children, Lonnie, will be just like us."

DINNER *at* AUNT CONNIE'S HOUSE

is based on my 1986 painted story quilt, "The Dinner Quilt." The painted story quilt is an art form I developed in 1983 that combines painting, sewing, and storytelling.

While *Dinner at Aunt Connie's House* shares many elements with "The Dinner Quilt," the story changed as it was transformed from a story for adult audiences to a story for children. I intended the original story for adults to recall their childhood memories of good times at festive dinners, with relatives and close friends, sharing family stories and delicious food. *Dinner at Aunt Connie's House* includes all of the family members in "The Dinner Quilt" including the children Melody and Lonnie. But the twelve African-American women (Rosa Parks, Fannie Lou Hamer, Mary McCleod Bethune, Augusta Savage, Dorothy Dandridge, Zora Neale Hurston, Maria W. Stewart, Bessie Smith, Harriet Tubman, Sojourner Truth, Marian Anderson, and Madame C. J. Walker) who originally appeared in "The Dinner Quilt" only as names that Aunt Connie embroidered on her place mats have become portrait paintings who speak to Lonnie and Melody. I added this element of magic to commemorate the courage, vision, and creativity of women who have made great contributions to American history but have been largely unknown.

DINNER AT AUNT CONNIE'S HOUSE is an expression of my belief that art can be more than a picture on a wall—it can envision our history and illustrate proud events in people's lives. And what's more, it can be magical!

—Faith Ringgold, 1993

Faith Ringgold was born in Harlem in 1930. An artist of international renown, she began her career more than twenty-five years ago as a painter. In the early 1970s, inspired by fourteenth-century Tibetan *tankas*—paintings on fabric that were framed with brightly colored silk brocades—she began to experiment with painting on unstretched canvases framed in cloth. These works are what Ms. Ringgold calls her "early quilts." Inspired as well by African art, she experimented with soft sculpture forms and masks, mixing the sewing she learned from her mother, Willi Posey, who was a fashion designer and dressmarker, with traditional fine art forms she learned in school. Ms. Ringgold made her first quilt, "Echoes of Harlem," in 1980, in collaboration with her mother.

Today, Faith Ringgold is best known for her painted story quilts—art that combines painting, quilted fabric, and storytelling. "The Dinner Quilt," upon which *Dinner at Aunt Connie's House* is based, was created in 1986. It has been exhibited at major museums and is now housed in a private collection.

Faith Ringgold is married and has two daughters and three granddaughters. She is a professor of art at the University of California at San Diego, where she teaches for half the year. She has received more than twenty-five awards and honors for her art, including the Solomon R. Guggenheim Fellowship for painting and six honorary doctorates, one of which is from her alma mater, the City College of New York.

Her first book, *Tar Beach,* was a Caldecott Honor Book and winner of the Coretta Scott King Award for illustration, among numerous other honors. *Dinner at Aunt Connie's House* is Faith Ringgold's first book for Hyperion Books for Children.